AUG. 1999

Till Year's Good End

Till Year's Good End

A Calendar of Medieval Labors

by

W. Nikola-Lisa

illustrated by

Christopher Manson

Atheneum
Books *for* Young Readers

Atheneum Books for Young Readers
An imprint of Simon & Schuster Children's Publishing Division
1230 Avenue of the Americas
New York, New York 10020

Book design by Michael Nelson

Hand lettering by Bobbi Yoffee
The text of this book is set in Post Antiqua Medium.

First Edition
Printed in the United States of America
10 9 8 7 6 5 4 3 2 1

LIBRARY OF CONGRESS CATALOGING-IN-PUBLICATION DATA
Nikola-Lisa, W.
Till year's good end : a calendar of medieval labors / by W. Nikola-Lisa ;
illustrations by Christopher Manson.—1st ed.
p.   cm.
Summary: Presents farm activities, month by month, in
England during the Middle Ages.
ISBN 0-689-80020-7
1. Harvesting—England—Juvenile literature. 2. Planting time—England—
Juvenile literature. 3. Country life—England—Juvenile literature.
4. England—Social life and customs—1066–1485—Juvenile literature.
5. Middle Ages—Juvenile literature. [1. Civilization, Medieval. 2. Farm
life—England. 3. England—Social life and customs—1066–1485. 4. Months.]
I. Manson, Christopher, ill. II. Title.
GT5856.44.N56   1997
942.02—dc20
95-45822

→ *The illustrations were created in pen-and-ink and watercolor on Rieves BFK paper, and were inspired by illustrations in early printed books.*
The lettering for the couplets was designed especially for this book, based on traditional medieval Blackletter (Gothic) styles, and to conform
to the enclosure shapes drawn by the illustrator.

To an ordered life;
To Franny and Cecil

–W. N-L.

To my wife

–C. M.

Author's Note

The most popular books of the Middle Ages, the Books of Hours, recorded the medieval calendar of feasting and holy days. Lavishly illustrated, these prayer books for the wealthy also contained in their detailed pictures information about everyday life. Each book's illustrated calendar pages included the 365 feast days of the Church and the twelve signs of the zodiac with their monthly labors. These rural labors had to be completed in each season so that the lord and the peasant survived the cold winter months. Although the medieval agricultural year began in late September after the grain harvest, our book begins in January, the start of the calendar year today.

JANUARY
By the fire
I warm my hands,

During the Middle Ages, the typical medieval peasant was a tenant farmer who rented lands from a powerful landowner. Although he had his own hut, livestock, and several plots of land, he was required to pay an assortment of rents and to give much of his labor to the governing lord. Not only did he, and sometimes his entire family, have to work in the lord's fields two or three times

And gaze upon
yon frozen lands.

a week, but he also had to repair bridges, clear roads, and maintain buildings. January, still under the influence of the Christmas season, was generally a time of feasting, a time when peasants stayed indoors in front of a warm hearth and blazing fire.

FEBRUARY — **Hunting nets**

hough remaining indoors for most of the cold winter months, peasants were not idle. Many indoor activities took much of their time. These included repairing hunting nets, fashioning leather harnesses, sharpening knives and axes, fitting handles on scythes and sickles, making reed mats and baskets,

carving wooden spoons, platters, and bowls, and, of course, spinning flax and wool into thread to make new clothes. On milder days, when peasants could venture outdoors, there was firewood to gather, vines to prune, fences to mend, and livestock to feed.

MARCH

I till the earth first sign of spring,

nce spring had arrived, peasants took to the fields. A manorial estate was divided into the lord's demesne lands and the village's communal lands, which were subdivided into small strips that peasants worked individually. In the spring, when the ground needed to be plowed, everyone worked together sharing oxen and plow, cultivating the lord's fields first, and then their own. During the

And sow good seed while blackbirds sing.

late Middle Ages, a three-field system of crop rotation was used to increase crop production. In one field a cereal crop of rye or wheat was planted in autumn to be harvested in summer. In another field, crops of barley, oats, or millet were planted in the spring and harvested in the summer. A third field was left unplanted, or fallow, and was used to pasture sheep and cattle.

APRIL Sheds I patch; and ditches dig.

As the weather warmed, spring brought a host of other outdoor activities—cleaning ditches, repairing stream banks, mending fences, pruning trees, hauling timber, and fixing sheds. The raw material for most repair work was found close at hand—sticks, twigs, clay, mud, straw, sand, even animal hide and hair.

Most buildings were built using a "wattle-and-daub" technique where a tightly woven mesh of sticks and twigs (the wattle) was erected between timber supports, and covered with a mixture of clay, straw, and mud (the daub). A roof was made from straw thatching which was bundled and fixed firmly in place.

MAY   Sheep are herded

The sheep herds had increased during the early spring months with the birth of new lambs. Now they needed to be washed and sheared. This activity began after the lambs stopped nursing and continued throughout June. Sheep were valued for their fleece, meat, milk, skin, and manure. Peasants also had oxen, cows, pigs, goats, chickens, and geese. Horses, kept mostly by the nobility, were

to wash and shear, While swarming bees buzz ever near.

used for transportation rather than for work in the fields. Bees were kept in clay hives and prized for their honey and wax. When the bees swarmed from their hives, usually twice a year, workers clapped or beat metal objects together to get the swarm to settle in a new hive.

JUNE

Through hay-filled fields

I go a-mowing

The major activity in the fields during June was mowing the hay crop, which was planted in the meadowlands. This chore required many hands, and took several days. While men cut the hay with their two-handed scythes, women and children raked the hay into piles. At the end of the day, the hayward,

Till hayward's horn
I hear a·blowing.

a peasant who was responsible for watching the fields and the movement of farm animals, blew his horn to call the peasants in for a feast provided by the lord. After mowing all the lord's hay, peasant families turned to their own fields where the ripened hay stood waiting to be cut.

JULY   Thick rows of peas I hoe and weed.

fter the hay harvest, peasants began to harvest the "corn"—a term used for different types of grains, usually rye or wheat, both of which were important products in the Middle Ages. The bundled sheaves were left in the fields to dry over the next few weeks. When they were not harvesting the lord's corn, peasants spent what little time they had tending their own strips of communal land, and

Vile brine I boil for salt I need.

weeding their garden plot, or "croft," where they grew leeks, onions, peas, and beans, among other things. Salt, an important ingredient for preserving meat and pickling vegetables, was mined from large pits. Chunks of salt, carried in sacks, were brought to the boiling-house where they were dissolved in water. After the water evaporated, the coarse salt crystals were dried and stored for later use.

AUGUST

Sheaves of barley, oats, and wheat

fter the bundled sheaves were dry, peasants took them to the granary where the corn was beaten with a flail to separate the grain from the stalk. To separate the chaff from the grain, it was winnowed with a fan or tossed lightly in the air. Although threshing continued throughout the month, the first

day of August was known as Lammas, or "loaf-mass," when peasants feasted on bread baked from the first grain harvest. The grain was ground into flour and used to make a thick, dark bread; the stems were gathered for thatch; and the chaff was mixed with hay for animal fodder.

SEPTEMBER

Orchards, too, give their fair share—

With the coming of autumn, the orchard fruit began to ripen. Apples, cherries, plums, and pears were the main cultivated fruits. Men and women harvested the orchards from tall ladders or by knocking the ripened fruit from the trees with long poles. Although some fruit was stored in cold cellars, much of it was dried for use during the winter months. Grapes on hillside

Apple, cherry, plum, and pear.

vineyards were ripening, too. After they were picked and carted to the winery, the grapes were pressed into juice which was placed in barrels where it fermented into wine for use throughout the year. Beer, wine, and ale were popular and probably safer to drink than the untreated water.

The long days of summer had passed, but the work did not ease. After the threshing and winnowing begun in August was completed, peasants had their grains ground at the mill owned by the governing lord. As no one else was allowed to own a mill, this insured the lord additional rents and fees. Although hunting was strictly regulated in the lord's forest, peasants were free

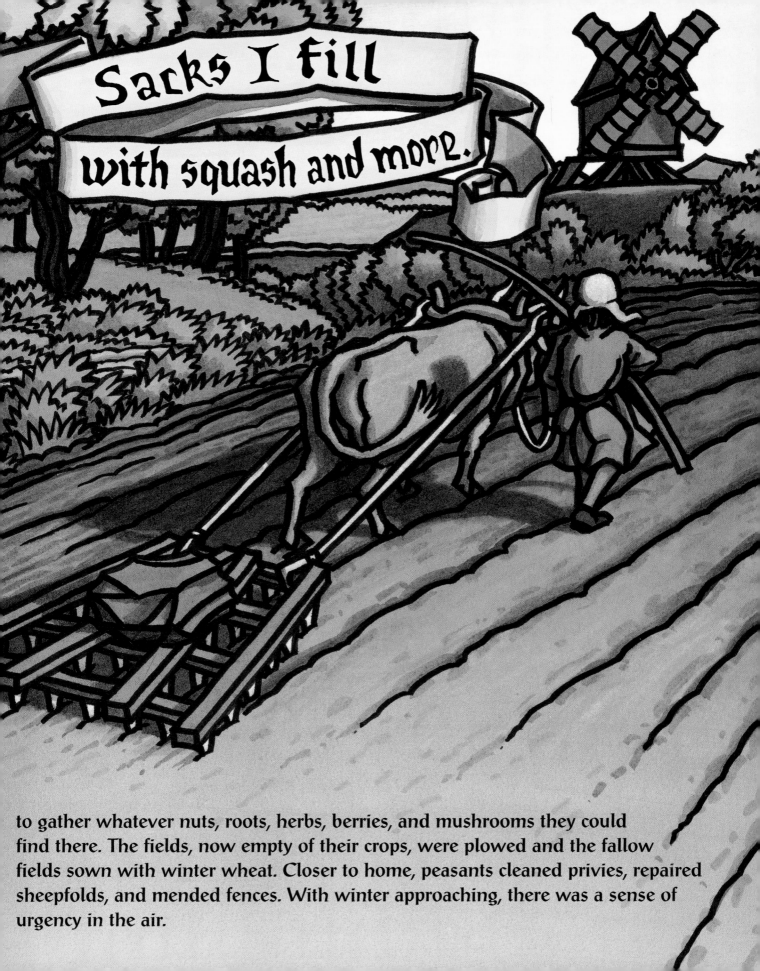

Sacks I fill
with squash and more.

to gather whatever nuts, roots, herbs, berries, and mushrooms they could find there. The fields, now empty of their crops, were plowed and the fallow fields sown with winter wheat. Closer to home, peasants cleaned privies, repaired sheepfolds, and mended fences. With winter approaching, there was a sense of urgency in the air.

NOVEMBER Wood I chop

Firewood, gathered since early fall, had to be split and stacked for winter use. Peasants were responsible not only for their own supply, but for that of their lord's as well. Pigs and oxen, fattened over the last few months, were slaughtered. The meat was smoked, salted, or dried into "jerky" to last through the cold winter months. Most animals raised through the warmer months

for long chill nights.

Pigs are fattened for feasting rites.

were slaughtered in the fall because it took much feed to keep them over
the winter. Willow twigs and reeds were collected for weaving baskets and mats;
rushes were gathered to make candlewicks; flax and hemp were processed
to make thread and rope.

DECEMBER
I hunt with Master, his dogs I tend—

lthough there was little work to do in the fields in December, still orchard trees needed trimming, grape vines needed pruning and staking for next year's harvest, and the clay banks of the mill pond, which had eroded during the wet months of autumn, needed to be rebuilt again. Hunting was popular, and

And rejoice full well
at year's good end.

necessary, but only lords and their attending servants were allowed to hunt in the royal forests. In the early months of autumn, deer, fox, and hare were hunted. In December, boar was hunted, a more difficult and dangerous task. At the end of the month, the great festival of Christmas was welcomed by one and all.